Ladybird books are widely available, but in case of
difficulty may be ordered by post or telephone from:

Ladybird Books – Cash Sales Department
Littlegate Road  Paignton  Devon TQ3 3BE
Telephone 0803 554761

A catalogue record for this book is available
from the British Library

Published by Ladybird Books Ltd  Loughborough  Leicestershire  UK

Printed in EC

# CAT SHOW CHAOS

Minnie the Minx was bored. Her cat Chester was bored, too. Slouched by the fire, they were idly watching a cat show competition on television. Minnie was not in the least interested in cat shows, but her eyes opened wide and her ears pricked up when she saw the winner receiving his cheque. How many thousands had the judge said? Minnie couldn't believe her ears but she was now VERY interested in cat shows.

Minnie quickly put on Mum's old raincoat, Dad's old motorcycle helmet, goggles and some old boots, followed by a thick pair of rubber gloves. Mum was VERY puzzled.

"What ARE you up to, Minx?" she snapped.

"Ever tried to give a cat a shampoo?" laughed Minnie, as she turned on the shower. The water hit Chester and he erupted into a screeching ball of wet fur.

"Now you'll know what to wear if you ever wash a moggy!" Minnie shouted to Mum.

But if Chester thought that his wash was bad, worse was to follow. Minnie knew that her cat wouldn't stand for a blow-dry, so she gave him the next best thing – a sharp blast of cold air from the open window.

Poor old Chester! He should have known better than to resist Minnie. He certainly was a sight to behold, but he didn't feel too good. He really was like the cat WITHOUT the cream!

Chester had thrown in the towel. He knew when a cat was beaten. Minnie quickly installed him in a 'poodle parlour' chair and set to work to transform him into the best-groomed cat in town.

Although Chester didn't think so, the results were truly magnificent and Minnie was as pleased as Punch. She knew a winner when she saw one – Chester was ready for stardom!

There was no time to lose. Chester was entered for the nearest cat show at the double! Held aloft on a velvet cushion, Chester felt like Cinderella heading for the ball.

When they arrived, the sight of all the model moggies stopped Minnie in her tracks. There were cats EVERYWHERE! Black cats and white cats, striped cats and spotted cats, Siamese, Persian, Manx… and there was Chester!

Minnie knew who was going to win!

Judging was going to take a very long time. There were just so many, many beautiful moggies. Minnie pondered for a moment… if only some of the cats WEREN'T so smart, life would be much easier.

"Chester," she whispered, "it's time to cut down the size of the opposition!"

TWANG! Chester shot down the table like a cannonball. The only difference was that THIS cannonball had claws. Suddenly, the air was filled with the flying fur of several very ruffled pedigree pussycats.

Minnie the Minx was right. It was easier for the judges now. In fact, it was TOO easy. Chester was the only unruffled cat in sight. Some of the other contestants had lost half their fur and some had even lost their wigs. To the judges they looked like the scruffiest collection of alley cats ever assembled.

The first part of the cat show only had one possible winner... Chester was on the ladder to success!

The next part of the show was a very difficult one to judge. The judges were looking for bright eyes, good bone structure and good teeth – something that Chester didn't have. Too much fish and chips had taken the gloss off Minnie's moggy's molars.

But Minnie had a plan. She also had a set of joke teeth up her sleeve and when Chester popped them into his mouth, the contest was as good as over. The 'tooth' of the matter was that all the other cats felt down in the mouth.

There was but one thing left for the judges to decide. Which cat behaved the best when there were lots of distractions? Now, there was only ever going to be one winner here. Chester had had so many distractions in his life that NOTHING really upset him. He was definitely the coolest cat in town.

And so it was that Minnie's cat Chester took first prize at the show. Minnie, sadly, was less than impressed with the winner's spoils.

"Chester, we are NOT amused!" she grumbled.

Robbed of their expected cash pay-out, Minnie and Chester decided to give the cat show judges something they'd always remember... a good old-fashioned cat fight! Chester's raking claws released the contestants from their cages and the fight was on!

To tell the truth, the other cats needed no persuasion to join in. After all, they enjoyed this sort of thing MUCH more than strutting about in ribbons and bows.

In seconds the hall was like a battlefield.

All too soon, it seemed, the cat fight was over. It didn't need the judges to decide who was the winner. One judge did, in fact, have the strength to wave a white flag from his position on top of the heap.

It was time to go. Minnie and Chester fled from the hall, howling like scalded cats. It really had been a show to remember.

Chester, proud as could be, clutched the winner's rosette in his paw.

Minnie's mum, however, was not at all impressed by the rosette. What impressed her more was the sight of her dear daughter's tattered clothes.

"Just look at you!" she roared. "You're like something that the cat dragged in! You're not coming in here like that, my girl!"

And so it was that Minnie found herself locked out, howling at the moon. But it wasn't long before Mum let her in again. She just couldn't stand Minnie's CAT-ERWAULING!